'SNURTLE'

By

Baruch Inbar

This book is dedicated to my dear mother, Sophia, whose wisdom, inspiration and eternal love, made me who I am today. I love you mom!

...And, This book is also dedicated to all the SNURTLES out there, who fiercely stand up in the face of rejection, separation and condemnation.

This is the story of a fellow named SNURTLE,

Whose mom is a snail and his dad is...a turtle!

3

When his parents got married, they got into trouble:

No one has ever seen such a strange looking couple!

4

Their life was
no walk in the
park,

They constantly
felt like they
had some
strange mark.

WELCOME TO THE
NOAH'S ARK
PARK

6

After SNURTLE was born, within less than two weeks,

The neighbors came over and said they were freaks!

8

EVICTION NOTICE!

We, the people of this town hereby voted for the immediate eviction of your property from our land. We decided that we no longer desire your

...to evict the land otherwise...

Signed by the town's lawyer,

oug S. Barker

9

They explained that only one species
                    Can live with it's kind

"Therefore, your residence here
                    Is forever denied!"

So SNURTLE's parents had
no choice but to leave,

And such a decision was hard to
conceive.

They packed up
their stuff and
drove out of
reach,

Where no one
would judge
them, hurt them,
or preach.

14

15

They thought that
there must be
others, just like
them,

Who would gladly
accept, not reject or
condemn.

16

Throughout the
hard journey their
hope
remained strong

That true friends
and help would
appear before long.

18

WELCOME HOME!

19

After one year of wandering and
searching for home,

They stopped for a rest next to an
odd looking dome.

SNURTLE approached
it, hearing laughter
and glee,

He peeked through the
window, and was
amazed to see:

The most strange-looking
creatures were dancing
and singing

They all looked so happy
- Snurtle's heart began
tingling.

24

Suddenly the door
opened, giving
Snurtle such a fright

Though he needn't
have feared, the
greeter was kind and
polite

26

She smiled and
exclaimed "My name
is Rhinaroo"

My dad is a Rhino
and my mom is a
Kangaroo

Won't you please come in
and meet the whole crew

You are very welcome and
your family is, too!

Snurtle and his parents eagerly joined the celebration

Their dreams had come true, they found their dream destination

The party at the dome lasted from dusk until dawn,

When new friends arrive, that's a time to shine on!

"This dome is a place
of peace and love",
Said a fellow named
CROWVE,

Who as you probably
guessed, is half crow
and half...dove!

So if you are seeking love and
a caring embrace

Look up those side roads for
that magical place

That is the special spot where it's safe to be you

That's the community that feels welcoming and true.

40

It's a village where
celebration is a daily
routine,

Where no one is weird,
even if you are orange,
purple or green.

42

Whoever you are is perfect
and true,

So stick with those that think
this way too!

44

THE END...

OR

THE BEGINNING?...